Author's note: This story is probably a metaphor for something. A tip of my hat, as usual, to my brilliant and patient art and editorial team: Nancy Paulsen, Cecilia Yung, Richard Amari and Sara Kreger.

G. P. PUTNAM'S SONS

A division of Penguin Young Readers Group. Published by The Penguin Group. Penguin Group (USA) Inc., 375 Hudson Street, New York, NY 10014, U.S.A. Penguin Group (Canada), 90 Eglinton Avenue East, Suite 700, Toronto, Ontario M4P 2Y3, Canada (a division of Pearson Penguin Canada Inc.). Penguin Books Ltd, 80 Strand, London WC2R 0RL, England. Penguin Ireland, 25 St. Stephen's Green, Dublin 2, Ireland (a division of Penguin Books Ltd.). Penguin Group (Australia), 250 Camberwell Road, Camberwell, Victoria 3124, Australia (a division of Pearson Australia Group Pty Ltd). Penguin Books India Pvt Ltd, 11 Community Centre, Panchsheel Park, New Delhi - 110 017, India. Penguin Group (NZ), 67 Apollo Drive, Rosedale, North Shore 0632, New Zealand (a division of Pearson New Zealand Ltd). Penguin Books (South Africa) (Pty) Ltd, 24 Sturdee Avenue, Rosebank, Johannesburg 2196, South Africa. Penguin Books Ltd, Registered Offices: 80 Strand, London WC2R 0RL, England.

Published simultaneously in Canada.

Manufactured in China by South China Printing Co. Ltd.

Text set in Layout Regular.

The art was done with black pencil and charcoal on newsprint. Color was added digitally.

Library of Congress Cataloging-in-Publication Data

Horowitz, Dave, 1970– Buy my hats! / Dave Horowitz. p. cm. Summary: Frank and Carl try to figure out why no one wants to buy their hats while other vendors are attracting many customers. [1. Retail trade—Fiction. 2. Hats—Fiction. 3. Animals—Fiction.] I. Title.

PZ7.H78755Buy 2010 [E]—dc22 2009022192

ISBN 978-0-399-25275-4

1 3 5 7 9 10 8 6 4 2

FOR MY FATHER,
the greatest businessman I know.
CUP O' MUD
Mmm...
CUP O' MUD
Mmm...
BUY MY HATS!

BUY MY HATS!
HATS
UP
$10
PAINT

Monday

Down at the City Market, Frank and Carl got ready to sell some hats.

"Step right up," said Carl. "Who wants to buy a hat?"

But nobody did.

Frank and Carl sold only **ONE** hat all day.

SKATE MONKEY
SKATEBOARDS
Thanks Ma'am.
BAD 2 DA BONK
Sweet!

BUY MY HATS!
SKATE MONKEY
SKATEBOARDS
Have fun.
Joy!
$10
SKATE
It's FUN
Ta dum.
weeee...
Look at me.
ONE HAT SOLD TO HIM.

The Blue Monkey sold about seventy-five skateboards.

"What's your secret?" Frank asked.

"Duh," said the Monkey. "I sell skateboards. Everybody likes skateboards."

I'm parched.
$10
$8
Mmm... Mud.

"Maybe we should sell skateboards," said Frank.

"We don't have any skateboards," said Carl. "We only have hats."

"Oh yeah," said Frank.

Along came Mister Pig.

“Who in their right mind would buy a Cup o’ Mud?” whispered Carl.

As it turned out, everyone wanted a cup. There was a line around the block.

I want a grande.
Mmm
I want a medium.
I want a small.
CUP O' MUD™

Frank and Carl didn't sell a single hat that day.

"What's your secret?" Frank asked.

"Advertising," said Mister Pig. "Have you ever seen such advertising? Everyone knows Cup o' Mud™!"

CUP O' MUD™
Mmm...
CUP O'MUD
MY NAME IS MUD
CUP O' MUD
Mmm MUD
Mmmm...
WOO HOO!
Hey—this is actually kind of gross.

Wednesday

“We need better advertising,” said Frank.

Carl got out his trusty paintbrush.

“There,” he said. “That ought to do it.”

BUY MY HATS!
THEY'RE HAT-TASTIC!
?
$8
$5
PAIN

But no one even noticed his handiwork. Across the way, Big Ox was selling remote control robot cell phones.

"What in the world is a remote control robot cell phone?" said Frank.

BUY MY HATS!
THEY'RE HAT-TASTIC!
yeah- I'm at the market.
Hey Mom, Do I like milk?
$10
$8
$5
oh really...? you don't say...
Hello?
Who?
What?
where?
Hello?
oh yeah— So I sez to her, hey Myrtle, where ever did you get that dress, and those shoes? And so she says, none of my business. Can you imagine ...?
ZZZZ

Whatever they were, Big Ox sold a hundred of them. Frank and Carl sold **ZERO** hats all day.

"What's your secret?" Frank asked.

"Are you kidding?" said Biggie. "These are new and exciting, man. They practically sell themselves."

Made in USA

Thursday

"Do you think our hats are new and exciting?" asked Frank.

"What do **YOU** think?" said Carl.

HATS!
THEY'RE HAT-TASTIC!
Mmmm...
Ug.
This stinks.
RING! RING!
ONLY $3!
Nice hat!
HA HA HA... Looks good on YOU though.

This turned out to be their worst day yet. What could be worse than selling **ZERO** hats?

Well, the kid they sold a hat to on Monday came back. He wanted a refund.

Friday

"I don't get it," said Frank. "Why doesn't anybody want to buy a hat?"

"How should I know?" said Carl. "Maybe folks just don't need hats."

THEY
HAT-
Sob
$1

Just then, there was a flash of lightning, and it started to rain.

"You've gotta be kidding me!" said Frank.

"We're ruined," said Carl.

$1
$10

BUY MY HATS!
THEY'RE RAINPROOF
HAT-TASTIC!
$10 $10
$8
$5
ONLY $3!

But then a funny thing happened. Suddenly everyone wanted a hat.

"We sure are great salesmen," said Frank. "I wonder what our secret is."

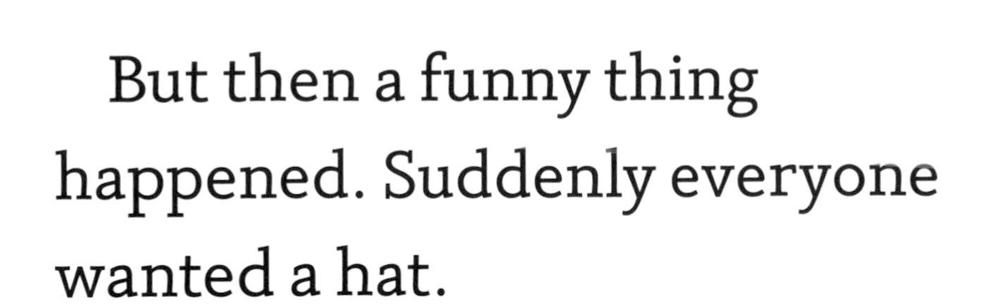

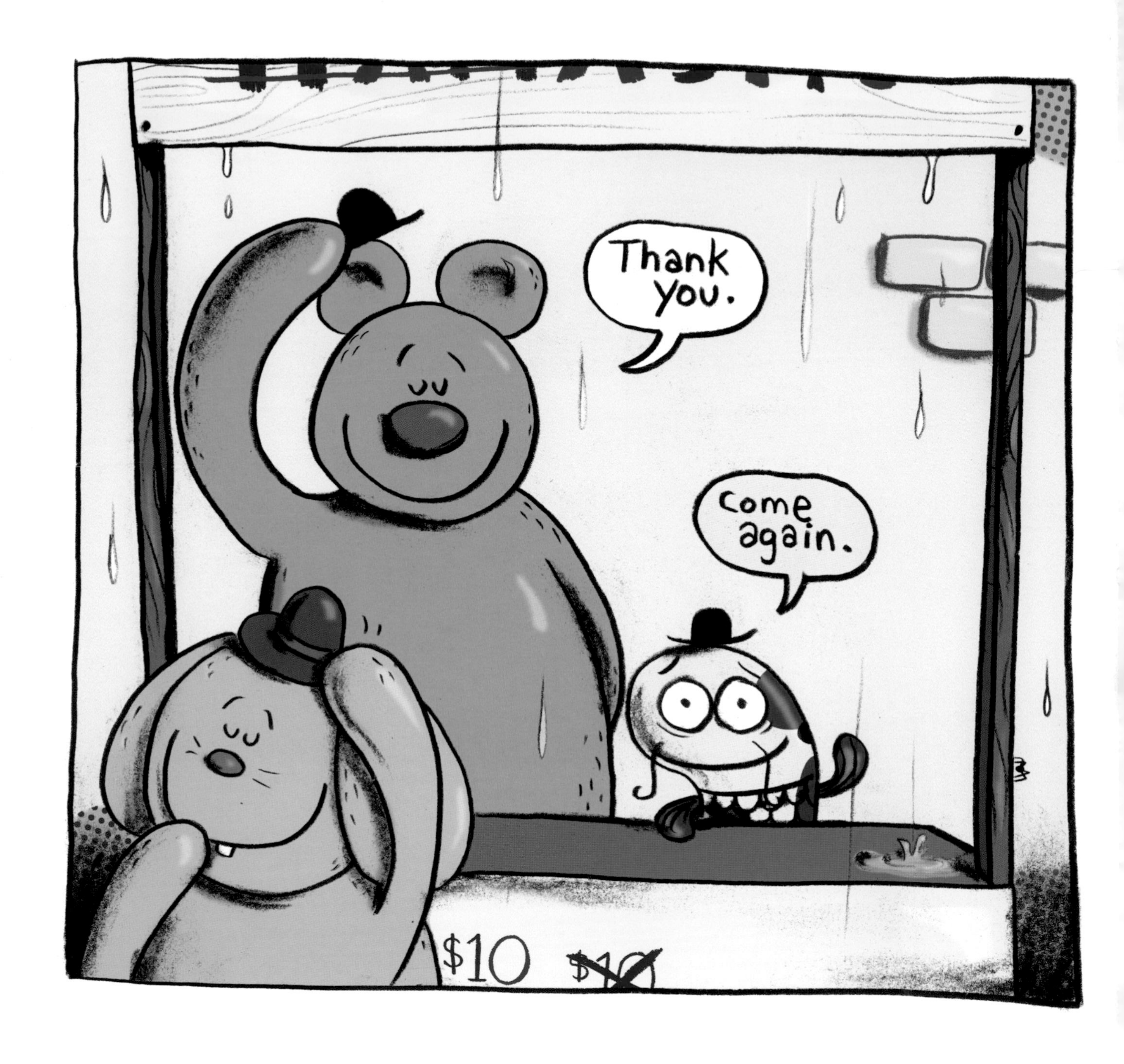

"I don't know," said Carl. "But next week, let's sell umbrellas, too."

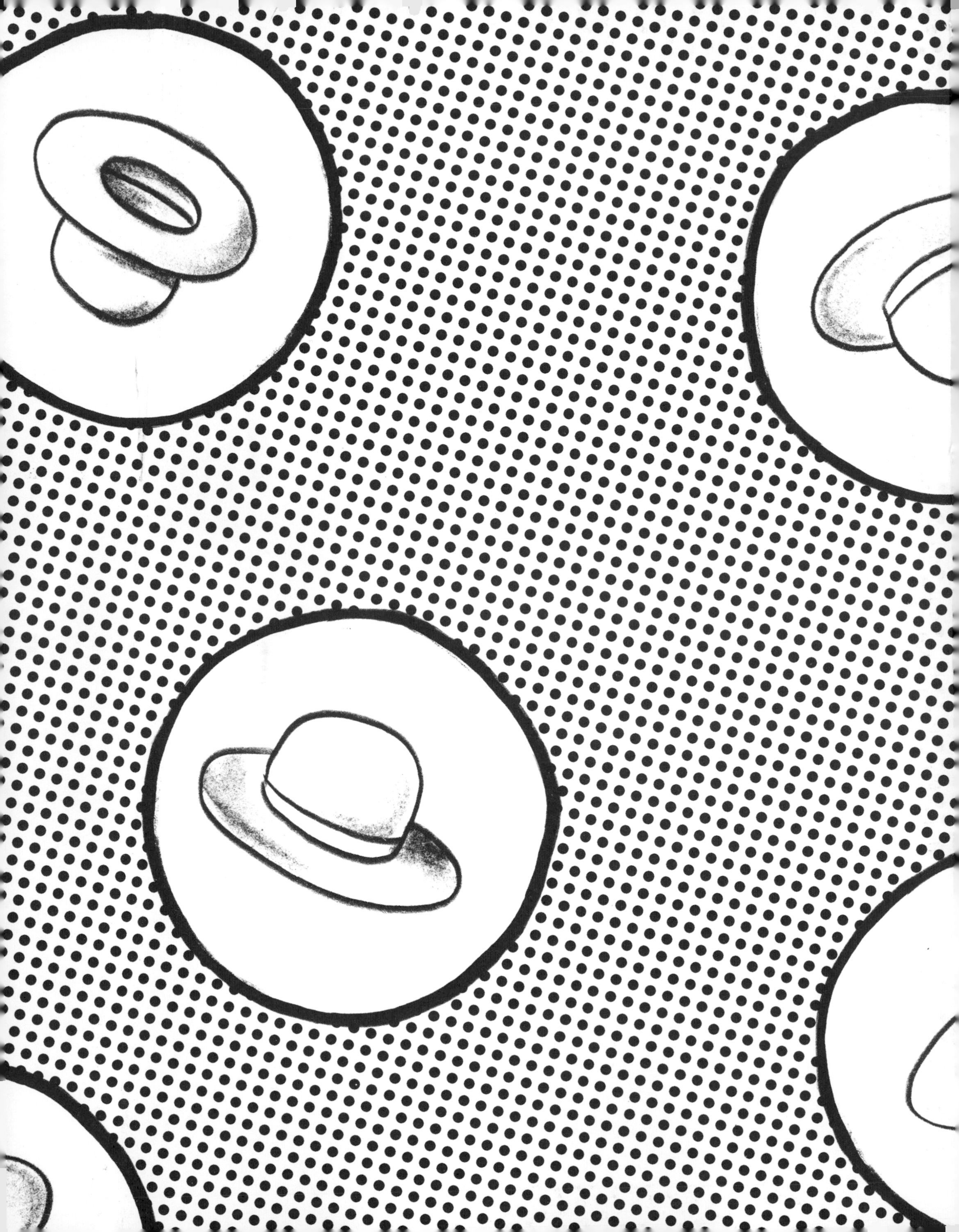